DATE DUE

E
T Tuxworth, Nicola
   Splish, splash : a very . . .

M.A. JONES ELEMENTARY

Splish, Splash

★ A very first picture book ★

The original publishers would like to thank Mark Bloodworth,
Freddy Cassford, Alice Crawley, Lauren Ferguson, Safari George, Saffron
George, Jasmine Haynes, Joseph Haynes, Erin Hoel, Charlotte Holden, Jack Matthews,
Megan Orr, Jimmy Pain, Philip Quach, Eloise Shepherd, and Nicola Tuxworth for
modeling for this book.

For a free color catalog describing Gareth Stevens Publishing's list of high-quality books and multimedia programs, call 1-800-542-2595 (USA) or 1-800-461-9120 (Canada). Gareth Stevens Publishing's Fax: (414) 225-0377.

Library of Congress Cataloging-in-Publication Data

Tuxworth, Nicola.
    Splish, splash: a very first picture book / Nicola Tuxworth.
      p. cm. — (Pictures and words)
    Includes bibliographical references and index.
    Summary: Photographs and simple text describe many ways a group
of young children use and have fun with water.
    ISBN 0-8368-2433-4 (lib. bdg.)
    [1. Water—Fiction.] I. Title. II. Series.
    PZ7.T887Sp   1999
    [E]—dc21   99-13422

This North American edition first published in 1999 by
Gareth Stevens Publishing
1555 North RiverCenter Drive, Suite 201
Milwaukee, WI 53212 USA

Original edition © 1997 by Anness Publishing Limited. First published in 1997 by Lorenz Books, an imprint of Anness Publishing Inc., New York, New York. This U.S. edition © 1999 by Gareth Stevens, Inc. Additional end matter © 1999 by Gareth Stevens, Inc.

Managing editor: Sue Grabham
Special photography: John Freeman
Stylist: Thomasina Smith
Design and typesetting: Michael Leaman Design Partnership

Picture credits: Papilio Photography: mute swan; Zefa Picture Library (UK) Ltd.: elephant, dog, and hippopotamus.

Printed in Mexico

1 2 3 4 5 6 7 8 9 03 02 01 00 99

PICTURES & WORDS

Splish, Splash

★ A very first picture book ★

Nicola Tuxworth

Gareth Stevens Publishing
MILWAUKEE

That car needs
a good cleaning...

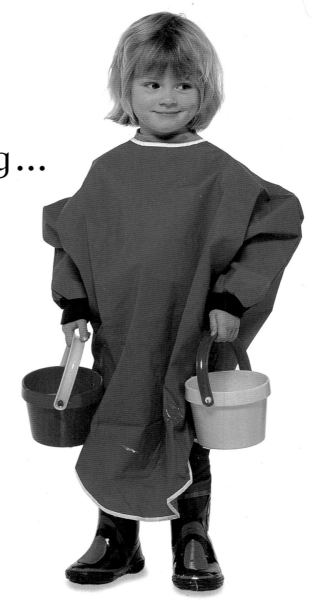

...with lots of
soapy water.

4

Splish,
splosh,
splash.

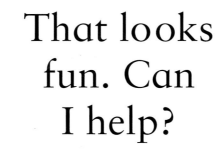

That looks
fun. Can
I help?

We're ready
to play in
the rain.

Wheee!
I'm jumping
in a puddle.

Whoops...

...I'm sitting
in a puddle!

7

I can wash
myself.

Look at my
new hairdo!

Where did those three ducks go?

9

Do you think we'll catch anything today?

Look!
We both
caught
whoppers!

Let's take
them home
for supper.

We're going to
water the flowers.

This sunflower needs
a lot of water.

My watering can
is empty.

13

We like splishing
and splashing with
our hands.

We like sploshing with our feet.

Let's get
Mom
all wet!

Oh, no...

16

...I'm all wet!

We're going
to feed the
ducks.

Mmm...
this tastes nice!

You look
hungry!

We like splishing and splashing, too!

Swish, swash with my trunk.

Paddle, paddle with my paws.

Whoosh,
swoosh
with my
wings.

Gargle,
gargle
with my
mouth.

You should see the
one that got away!

Questions for Discussion

1. Name five different kinds of animals that live in the water. What special body parts do these animals have that help them survive in the water?

2. Besides water, what do plants need to grow?

3. Name some objects that float in water. Name some objects that sink in water.

4. What happens to the water in a puddle when it dries up? Where does it go after that? Does it ever turn into a puddle again?

5. To keep yourself dry when it is raining, what kinds of clothes do you wear? What clothes do you wear when the weather is very cold? What do you wear during hot weather?

More Books to Read

All About Water. Melvin Berger (Scholastic)

At the Pond. Look Once, Look Again (series). David M. Schwartz (Gareth Stevens)

My Boat. First Step Science (series). Kay Davies and Wendy Oldfield (Gareth Stevens)

Puddles and Pond. Rose Wyler (J. Messner)

Rain Drop Splash. Alvin R. Tresselt (Mulberry Books)

Rupert's Big Splash: An Early Learner Book About Water. Bob Graham (Gallery Books)

Water Voices. Toby Speed (G. P. Putnam's Sons)

Videos

Air and Water Wizardry.
  (Playhouse Video)

Ask Oscar: Water.
  (Landmark Films)

Rainy Day Adventure.
  (Discovery Music)

Water and Weather.
  (Prism Entertainment)

Web Sites

www.ctw.org/preschool/
  games/play/

www.fi.edu/city/water

Some web sites stay current longer than others. For further web sites, use your search engines to locate the following topics: *fishing, rain, rain cycle, science, science experiments,* and *water.*

Glossary-Index

gargle: to rinse the throat and mouth with a liquid, such as water or a mouthwash. (p. 21)

hairdo: the way hair is arranged by combing, cutting, or styling. (p. 8)

puddle: a small pool of water or other liquid. (p. 7)

sunflower: a flower with yellow petals and a dark center. (p. 13)

swish: to move with a soft, hissing sound. (p. 20)

trunk: the long, flexible snout of an elephant. (p. 20)

whoppers: objects that are very large. (p. 11)